BLIZZARDS!
AND ICE STORMS

BLIZZARDS!
AND ICE STORMS

by Maria Rosado

SIMON SPOTLIGHT

ACKNOWLEDGMENTS

The publisher is grateful to the following individuals for permission to reproduce their photographs:

Cover and insert: David C. Smith and Doug Bradley. Interior photos: Doug Bradley; David Swang; Niagara Mohawk, Canada; and NCDC/NOAA. Snowflake photomicrographs by Wilson A. Bentley (1865-1931), courtesy Jericho Historical Society. American memory accounts and photographs courtesy of the Library of Congress.

Special thanks to the following for permission to use the first-hand accounts found in chapter five: The Dilkie family and Corey Aist and his dog, Vanilla Bean, of Alaska Search & Rescue Dogs in Anchorage. For use of the online ice storm accounts, thanks to Matthew Killen, the creator; Jim Moulton; The Community of Learners, online host; and the children of the Northeast who contributed.

For their assistance with research, thanks also to George Walters, Shawn Green and the Potomac Appalachian Trail Club; Kenneth G. Libbrecht at Caltech; and Ray Miglionico, archivist.

 SIMON SPOTLIGHT

An imprint of Simon & Schuster Children's Publishing Division
1230 Avenue of the Americas, New York, New York 10020
Copyright © 1999 by The Weather Channel, Inc.
All rights reserved. "The Weather Channel" is a registered trademark
of The Weather Channel, Inc. used under license.
All rights reserved including the right of reproduction
in whole or in part in any form.
SIMON SPOTLIGHT and colophon are registered trademarks of
Simon & Schuster.
Manufactured in the United States of America
First Edition 10 9 8 7 6 5 4 3 2
Rosado, Maria, 1963-
Blizzards! and ice storms! / by Maria Rosado.
p. cm.
Includes index.
Summary: Identifies blizzards and ice storms, their causes,
and effects. Includes safety tips, eyewitness accounts, and
Web site addresses.
ISBN 0-689-82016-X (pbk.)
1. Blizzards—Juvenile literature. 2. Ice storms—Juvenile literature.
[1. Blizzards. 2. Ice Storms.] I. Title
QC926.37.R67 1999
551.55'5—dc21   99-31150 CIP

Contents

1

Winter Storm Warning!

On the streets of New York City, newsboys call out the forecast from the weekend papers they wave at passersby: "Fair weather on Monday!" They don't know yet that the forecast they're selling is wrong—dead wrong. In reality, the city will soon be locked in the frozen grip of "The Blizzard of 1888," one of the worst storms in U.S. history.

Silent But Deadly

The rain changes to snow about ten minutes after midnight on Monday morning, March 12th. By daybreak, the city is already buried under ten inches of snow. The wind roars down the cobblestone streets at twice the speed of the fastest steam locomotive.

Driven by these fierce gusts, snow is swept from one side of the street to the other, forming towering drifts. Over the next couple of days, the drifts climb higher and higher—five feet, ten feet, twenty feet—covering windows up to the second floor of apartment buildings and completely blocking many doors. People must tunnel their way out to the street.

On the second day of the storm, temperatures have dropped to nearly zero. Those too poor to buy fuel for their stoves shudder without heat and dozens freeze in their own homes, waiting for the snow to stop.

Everywhere in the city, water pipes burst when water freezes inside them, while telegraph poles topple and split. Some rooftops buckle under the weight of all the snow.

Terror at Sea

Up and down the Atlantic shoreline, from the coasts of Maine to Virginia, 200 tugboats, schooners, and steamships swamp or sink to the bottom of the sea. A gale-force wind whips the sea into waves four

KID QUIZ

Q: How did blizzards get their name?

A: For a long time. the word blizzard was used to describe either a punch or a burst of rifle shot. Then. on March 14. 1870. a reporter used it in his story about a fierce snowstorm that blasted through Minnesota and Iowa. It was the first time anyone used the word "blizzard" to write about snowy weather.

stories tall. Towering masts split like matchsticks and thick iron anchor chains snap under the strain. Ships remaining afloat buck like rodeo horses, pitching men overboard.

Snow On the Tracks

Four people are killed when a railway train on its way uptown to Harlem tries to slam its way through the snow and derails. Meanwhile, high above the street, the city's famous elevated trains plow to a stop on their own snow-packed tracks leaving hundreds of unlucky passengers trapped. When trains ahead are stalled, one engineer tries to stop but the train can't grip the icy rails. It collides with the train in front of it with a sound like thunder. By nightfall on Monday, not one train is moving in the city.

Meltdown

Before all the snow is cleared, people must dig tunnels into the two-story high drifts to let horse-drawn carriages drive through. In places, the drifts are so thick they can't be shoveled or thawed at all, even when men light fires to try to melt them from the inside out.

In the meantime, to get where they're going, people sled or ski through the streets.

Some thrill-seeking "commuters" walk

across the river between Manhattan and Brooklyn over a bridge of solid floating ice that is wedged for hours near the Brooklyn Bridge. Several thousand people make the crossing safely until the floating ice bridge starts to loosen with the high tide. A hundred or so are stranded as the ice floats away. Most jump to safety onto nearby piers. The last three men stranded on the ice are rescued by a tugboat.

Blowing Over

It is sundown March 14th, before the Blizzard of 1888 finally blows away from the northeast coast. Over 400 people have perished along the East Coast, 200 in New York City alone, most by exposure to the freezing cold. Outside the city, thousands of livestock have been killed by the icy temperatures. Millions of dollars are needed to repair buildings damaged by the blizzard's snow and wind.

When it is all over, a record-breaking twenty-one inches of snow blankets New York City, and it will be weeks before it is shoveled off most streets. No trains or delivery wagons can reach shops with supplies. As a result, shortages of food, water and fuel sweep the city.

That Was Then, This Is Now

Nowadays, a storm like the Blizzard of 1888 is not likely to strike without some kind of warning. Meteorologists can now identify the ingredients that will cook up a

KID QUIZ

Q: What is a snow squall?

A: Squalls are short-lived bursts of precipitation, which is the term for any form of water that falls from clouds to the ground. Squalls are accompanied by brief, strong gusty winds. Snow squalls can produce heavy snow and high winds but typically last less than half an hour.

storm long before it strikes. They then issue a forecast warning people about where and when it will arrive.

How Bad Can it Be?

Just how bad can a modern blizzard be? Take a look at the blizzard of 1993. Called "The Superstorm," it thundered up the eastern coastline, covering an area more than six times the size of a typical hurricane, whipping up tornadoes and flooding the coast. The Superstorm arrived on March 12th, 1993, exactly 105 years after the Blizzard of 1888. In all, twenty-two states were affected and more than half the U.S. population felt its effects first-hand. Total damage from the 1993 storm has been estimated at $6 billion. The storm cut off power to over three million people and forced every major airport on the East Coast to close—the only time in history that has ever happened.

You Say Blue Norther, I Say Nor'easter

The Blizzards of both 1888 and 1993 were "nor'easters," storms that rage across the states on the Eastern Seaboard and are named for the northeasterly winds that precede the passage of the storm's center. Winter weather that brews up in different regions can have other names:

• "Blue northers" deliver cold air across the Southern Plains to Texas.

• "Arctic outbreaks" can bring record lows just about anywhere in the U.S.

• "Lake effect snow" is the name given to flakes that fall when cold air blows over large, relatively warm lakes. Though this occurs in other locations, areas near the Great Lakes are known for storms like these, which can result in persistent snow squalls and extremely large snow accumulations in localized areas.

- The "pineapple express," a corridor of clouds originating near Hawaii, indicates a weather pattern that can energize storms along the Pacific Coast.
- An "Alberta clipper" is a fast-moving storm that originates in western Canada.
- The "purga" is a violent blizzard that affects Siberia and southern Russia.

The Big Freeze

Ice storms are another of nature's frozen forces. In this type of storm, rain falling through a shallow layer of below-freezing air at ground level becomes supercooled, meaning its temperature falls below thirty-two degrees Fahrenheit but it remains liquid. The rain then freezes when it hits trees, streets, power lines, and houses, creating a coating of solid ice. This form of **precipitation** is known as freezing rain.

Fire and Ice

Ice Storm 1998, which struck the northeastern U.S. and southeastern Canada between January 5th and 9th of that year, provided a good example of the chaos that kind of weather can bring. Branches cracked as the storm laid down layers of ice as hard as concrete. Ice weighed down power lines until wires tore free from telephone poles, causing explosions of sparks and flame.

As a result, electricity to 3.5 million people was cut off. Without power, there was no heat, running water, or electricity. Hundreds of people were forced to leave their frozen homes and move into shelters or barracks built by the National Guard. In some areas, power couldn't be restored for almost a month. In the end there was $2 billion in damage to Canada and $300 million in the U.S.

2

Brewing Up a Blizzard

Although many people use the term "blizzard" to describe any weather with a lot of snow, blizzards are really a special type of storm. For a snowstorm to be classified a blizzard, there are specific wind speeds and low visibility requirements it must meet. In a true **blizzard**, the combination of falling and/or blowing snow plus sustained winds or frequent gusts of at least thirty-five miles an hour must lower the visibility to 1/4 mile or less for at least three hours in a row. Temperatures well below thirty-two degrees are typically associated with blizzards, too.

But what makes a blizzard blow? How does it form? What makes a blizzard so bad? These are just a few of the questions about this form of winter storm that science is now able to answer.

Snow Blowers

Strangely enough, blizzard conditions can occur without any snow actually falling from the sky. Strong winds can blow previously dumped snow, reducing the visibility to create blizzard conditions. Antarctica, which has some of the worst blizzards in the world, actually only gets a few inches of snow each year. But incredibly cold temperatures mean the snow never melts. So when the wind blows, it's stirring up years' worth of old snow.

A Shift in the Stream

Nowadays, scientists can predict a blizzard just by looking for changes in wind patterns. First, meteorologists keep a weather-eye out for shifts in the jet stream.

A **jet stream** is a giant band of wind that travels at great speed at about 30,000 feet up in the air. It circles the globe, rushing generally eastward at speeds up to 200

Did You Know?

For years, scientists just guessed that something like the jet stream existed. During World War II, U.S. Army pilots proved that trips going from west to east were always quicker than trips going from east to west. The pilots knew that something had to be pushing the jet planes along and that it was probably a forceful stream of air. Nowadays, we measure the jet stream's winds using weather balloons. Scientists also can view the jet stream in satellite photographs taken from space.

miles per hour. The jet stream helps separate the cold air to the north from warmer air to the south. It shifts its position depending on the seasons, dipping south across the U.S. during winter and north during summer.

Weather Watch

An **air mass** is a large body of air with roughly the same temperature and humidity throughout. At any moment there are many air masses moving across the Earth. When two different air masses meet, they can cause all different kinds of weather.

The Front Lines

The battle line formed when two air masses meet is called a **front**. When a cold air mass meets a warm air mass, a giant pinwheel of air, called a depression or low **pressure system,** can form. When a low pressure system happens to be filled with clouds of **ice crystals,** it can become a snowstorm just like the ones that formed the blizzards in 1888 and 1993.

EXPERIMENTAL SCIENCE: UP, UP, AND AWAY

You may have done this experiment already—without even realizing that it demonstrates the way hot air rises.

You will need:
1 bottle or pan of bubble liquid
1 bubble-blowing wand

Choose a calm day, out of the way of wind and drafts. Dip the wand into the bubble liquid and gently blow a stream of bubbles straight ahead. Watch carefully! Which way do the bubbles move at first . . . up or down? You'll observe that they float up. That's because the bubbles are filled with air that's been heated by your breath. If you blow bubbles on a day that's colder, you will see that they rise even higher and faster. When the air inside the bubbles starts to cool down, the bubbles will begin to sink.

That's a Low Blow

An area of low air pressure (commonly

referred to as a "low") initially can form along a front as warmer, lighter air rises over colder, heavier air. The surrounding air spirals inward toward the center of low pressure, creating wind—a key ingredient for a blizzard. If the low pressure strengthens, the winds will increase. During the blizzard of 1993, winds gusted faster than eighty miles per hour.

Lift it Higher

Once you have wind, you need snow to make a blizzard form. What causes snow? Snow begins with moisture—lots and lots of microscopic **water vapor** molecules in the air. More moisture can exist in warm air than in cold air. Air with a lot of moisture content is said to have high humidity. As warm air begins to rise, it will lift up the moisture. But as that air rises higher and higher, it cools and the water vapor eventually turns into ice crystals . . . the beginnings of snow.

A Storm Is Born

In 1993, an area of low pressure drew huge amounts of evaporated water from over the Gulf of Mexico into its circulation. Then it moved to the northeast and picked up some more moisture from the Atlantic Ocean. When all that moisture was forced to rise over a very cold air mass to the north—BAM! A blizzard was born.

3

What Makes Snow?

To understand exactly how a blizzard is formed, you need to start with its tiniest part: ice crystals. Ice crystals are the building blocks for each flake of snow.

Having a Ball with Crystals

The flakes that fly during a storm had to go through many stages before they fall onto your mitten. Here's how nature builds a flake:

• Ice Crystal: Clouds form when air rises and cools and water vapor condenses into tiny drops of water around specks of dust floating in the air. If the air becomes cold enough, water droplets within the clouds are supercooled, meaning they remain liquid even at temperatures below thirty-two degrees Fahrenheit. If that supercooled water collides with certain airborne particles, or if the air becomes even colder, then the water will freeze, forming an ice crystal too tiny to see without a microscope.

• Flake: Ice crystals start out small, but they can rapidly grow as more water vapor changes directly to ice on them. An ice crystal can grow in other ways, too: As supercooled water droplets collect on top of an ice crystal and freeze, or as it collides and freezes together with another ice crystal, ice crystals can become larger. A snowflake is a cluster of many, many ice crystals.

• Snow: When flakes grow too heavy to float, they begin to fall. The weather phenomenon we know as snow is created when these flakes fall to the Earth's surface. On their journey downward, flakes can grow even bigger as more layers of supercooled water and more ice crystals are added. In a winter storm, millions of snowflakes can fall. Each snowflake can be made up of hundreds of thousands of ice crystals.

I'm Melting, I'm Melting!

As a flake falls, different things can happen to it. If it passes through a warm layer of air, the flake will melt back into a drop of water. If it stays in warm air the rest of the way down, the drop will become rain. When a drop passes through a mixture of layers, different weather can occur. For instance, when a flake melts it might pass through a shallow layer of cold air near the Earth's surface and become supercooled. If it then hits something on the ground that's freezing cold, it will turn into ice. This is called freezing rain or sometimes **glaze**. But if a cluster of ice crystals falls through cold air all the way down to the ground, it will reach the ground as snow.

The Snowflake Man

The person who took the very first photographs of ice crystals was Wilson Bentley, aka "The Snowflake Man." Bentley's fascination with snow began in 1880, when he was just fifteen and his mother gave him an old microscope. Plenty

KID QUIZ

Q: What is sleet?

A: Sleet is formed when a snowflake falls through a layer of warm air, melts, then freezes again before it hits the ground. Unlike snow, sleet doesn't stick when it hits the ground. Instead, it bounces off the ground because it has frozen into a tiny ball, called an "ice pellet."

of snow falls on Jericho, the town in Vermont where the Bentley family lived, so flakes were one of the first things the teenager looked at under his lens. As soon as he saw all those intricate patterns of ice crystals, Bentley wanted to capture those images forever and show other people the wonder of snow.

Later, Bentley's parents saved up enough money to buy him a camera. The camera did not allow him to capture what he saw under a microscope, however. So, at the age of twenty and after much experimentation, Bentley rigged up a special combination camera-microscope. Pictures

KID QUIZ

Q: How big can flakes get?

A: Your average snowflake isn't very big—just 1/4 inch across. about the width of a small paper clip. In colder climates. flakes tend to be even smaller. The biggest flakes have been measured at three to four inches across. roughly the length of a good-sized goldfish.

like Bentley's, taken using a microscope, are called **photomicrographs**. These pictures capture amazing details in the tiniest flakes of snow. By preserving actual snowflake images on film, Bentley was able to show the basic forms snowflakes could take and was able to prove to scientists that different types of weather could affect flake shapes.

Twin Peeks

There's a famous saying that "no two snowflakes are alike." The truth is, scientists don't know this for sure. Every snowflake is made up of many individual ice crystals, and each of those crystals has six sides. That adds up to billions of different possible variations. So the odds are slim that any snowflake has an exact twin. Wilson Bentley never found twin snowflakes among his thousands of flake photos.

Ice in Summer

Have you ever seen ice fall from the sky in the summer? Well, it seems strange, but a form of ice called **hail** can fall even in summer. Hail is generally formed inside a thundercloud, a place where the air lifts up and down like an elevator jerking out of control. Hail starts off in the same way a snowflake is formed, but ice pellets trapped inside thunderclouds get bounced up and down many times before they fall to the ground. Each time they bounce up and down, the ice pellet gets another coating of ice. Because hailstones get so big, they don't melt even when they fall through layers of warm air. Hail is primarily a spring and summertime weather phenomenon but it can fall any time of the year when thunderstorms are present.

Avalanche!

The science of snow also includes a study

Beautiful but dangerous: An ice storm freezes trees in Shenandoah National Park.

ce injures trees all along the Appalachian Trail after the storm in January 1998. Over eighteen million acres of U.S. forest are damaged.

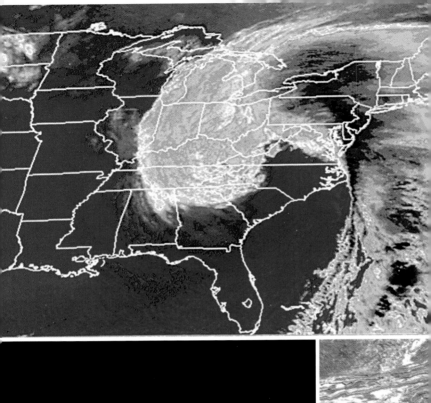

Snow cover over the Northeast after the blizzard of 1996.

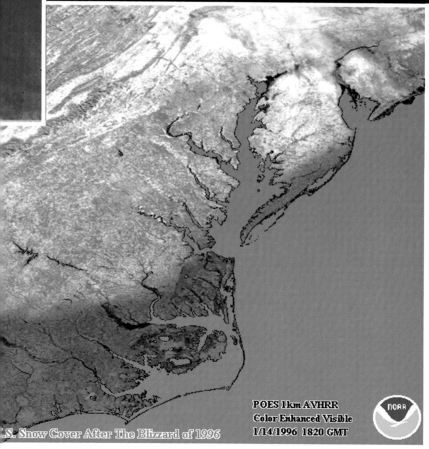

Infrared satellite image of "The Superstorm" during the early afternoon on March 13, 1993.

U.S. Snow Cover After The Blizzard of 1996

POES 1km AVHRR
Color Enhanced Visible
1/14/1996 1820 GMT

noaa

The January 1998 storm coats trees, streets, and power lines with two to four inches of ice.

Snowbanks reach 116 inches in Moorhead, Minnesota, after winter storms in 1997.

During the ice storm of 1998 falling poles rip down more than 1.8 million feet of power lines in the northern U.S. and Canada.

An example of the crystal s†
shape called "dendrite."

Temperature, moisture,
and air pressure help
shape snowflakes.

Flakes like this one have
almost perfect symmetry.

Some of the thousands of flakes photographed by
"Snowflake Bentley."

Star shapes like this form in air that is zero to twenty degrees.

Ice crystals are the building blocks of snowflakes like this one.

snowflakes are based on xagons, but they can take millions of shapes.

A tunnel dug through the snow in Farmington, Connecticut after the blizzard of 1888.

Snow whips down Wall Street in New York City during the blizzard of 1888.

Often, snow melts when the first flakes hit the ground, and when the temperature of the ground is above freezing. But snow can sometimes cool the earth as it melts. When the ground gets cold enough, the flakes that fall later in a storm don't melt, they stick.

of what happens when snow slides: Avalanche! An **avalanche** occurs when one layer of snow loses its "grip" on another, older layer of snow which is lying beneath it. Any kind of debris that slides down the side of a mountain or hill, and poses a danger as it falls, can be called an avalanche. As many as 90% of all reported avalanches happen during or immediately after snowstorms and blizzards, when new layers of snow have fallen on old ones.

The number of people caught in avalanches is growing. Why? Because more people are skiing, climbing, hiking, snow-mobiling, and snowboarding than ever before in history. With numbers of people on the slopes growing, the chances are higher that someone will be caught in an avalanche, or trigger a slide. Also, more trees are being cut down to make room for ski and snowboard runs, so it's easier for snow to slide longer distances, creating bigger and more dangerous avalanches.

Pressing the Trigger

Avalanches are most often triggered by people, when some movement causes an unstable section of snow to slide. But other factors can make an avalanche even more likely. One of them is the weather. Freezing temperatures and thawing temperatures can also loosen snow layers. An avalanche becomes even more likely when those warmer temperatures are quickly followed by a storm. If the snow falls faster than one inch every hour it creates a heavy, slippery layer on top of the snow that melted from the thaw. That top layer of heavy snow may start to slide.

Snowpack is another factor. That's the word scientists use to describe the amount of snow on the ground in any one place and the condition of that snow. To find out the condition of a snowpack, researchers take a snow sample from a specific location. They use a long, hollow pole to spear a column of snow many inches deep. Then they slide the column of snow out from the center of the pole and take a look at the layers.

Did You Know?

Deep snow isn't all bad. Believe it or not, snow keeps plants and animals warm. It acts as a blanket, insulating seeds, plant roots, and the burrows of small animals from the freezing cold above.

4

Frozen in Time

Blizzards and other types of icy weather have left a trail of destruction through the decades. This timeline shows that every generation seems to have its share of snowy disasters.

1895 - An unusual blizzard drops up to two feet of snow along the Texas and Louisiana Gulf Coast.

1899 - A great outbreak of cold air brings

the coldest morning in history to the southern plains and southeast United States. Snow and high winds create blizzard conditions in New Orleans and northern Florida. Snow falls in Fort Myers, Florida, the farthest south snow has fallen in the continental United States up to this point.

1932 - Two inches of snow falls in downtown Los Angeles.

1947 - New York City's biggest snowstorm on record dumps 26.4 inches of snow, over five inches more than what fell during the Blizzard of 1888.

1950 - A storm known as "The Appalachian Storm" brought blizzard conditions on Thanksgiving Day to much of the Midwest and parts of the East. Up to sixty-two inches of snow fell in West Virginia while 100-mile-per-hour wind gusts caused coastal flooding from New Jersey to New England.

1967 - One of the worst blizzards to ever strike an area within the Arctic Circle hits not long after pilot Robert Gauchie's plane is forced down for lack of fuel. He survives 58 days of raging storms by staying bundled under six sleeping bags in his plane until he is rescued—the record for winter wilderness survival.

1969 - People in New York are so furious with mayor John Lindsay's slow action to clean up after a blizzard, he loses his next election. The storm is later named "The Lindsay Storm" after him.

1970 - The largest hailstone ever documented falls during a storm in Coffeyville, Kansas. It weighs over 1 1/2 pounds and measures more than 5 1/2 inches across.

1977 - A new airport designed to brave the worst blizzards opens in Colorado. It is almost immediately shut down by snows from the next bad storm, stranding 2,000 angry passengers.

1977 - Buffalo, New York struggles through forty straight days of snowfall and then is hit by a big blizzard. It is the first city in U.S. history to be declared a Federal Disaster Area due to snow.

1978 - The Governor of Massachusetts outlaws travel for a week when Boston is covered with more than twenty-seven inches of snow in "The Great New England Blizzard."

1996 - A blizzard on January 7th and 8th drops nearly two feet of snow on New York City and Washington, D.C. The whole Federal Government is shut down for a day. Meanwhile, seven campers in Virginia's Shenandoah National Park are trapped in the wilderness for days by the blizzard. Food and water are dropped to them by helicopter.

1997 - Numerous blizzards and other heavy snowstorms hit the area around the Red River, which runs through the upper Midwest. When all the snow finally melts, towns from Canada to Minnesota are covered in mud and debris from the resulting flood. Whole houses are swept away and hundreds of thousands of people are forced to evacuate their homes.

5

They Lived to Tell

Snow may look beautiful—but it can be very dangerous. Here are some stories of people who survived an encounter with one of winter's most wicked extremes.

School Can be Deadly

During the winter of the infamous Blizzard of 1888, another blizzard struck with fury in the Dakotas, Montana, Nebraska, and Minnesota. O. W. Meier was fifteen years old when he and his two younger brothers battled that blizzard in Lincoln, Nebraska. Here's what it was like for Meier and his brothers, stranded by the storm in their school far from home:

Beautiful big white flakes were falling fast that morning of the fateful day. At the last recess, the snow was about two feet deep. As swiftly as lightning, the storm struck the north side of the schoolhouse. The whole building shivered and quaked.

In an instant the room became black as night. The teacher said. "Those who live south may put on their coats and go, but the rest of you must stay here in this house."

We had not gone [16.5 feet] when we found ourselves in a heavy drift of snow. We took hold of each others' hands [and] pulled ourselves out. The cold north wind blew us a half mile south. My brothers and I could not walk through the deep snow in the road, so we [walked] down the rows of corn stalks to keep from losing ourselves till we reached our pasture fence. Walter was too short to wade the deep snow in the field, so Henry and I dragged him over the top.

For nearly a mile we followed the fence till we reached the corral and pens. The roaring wind and stifling snow blinded us so that we had to feel through the yard to the door of our house. Pa was shaking the ice and snow from his coat and boots. He had gone out to meet us but was forced back by the storm.

That was an awful night on the open Plains. Many teachers and school children lost their lives in that blinding storm, while trying to find their way home. The blizzard of 1888 has not been forgotten.

—Excerpted from *American Life Histories: Manuscripts from the Federal Writers' Project, 1936-1940*

Snow Job

People lost in the snow stand a better chance of surviving today than they did back in 1888, thanks to people like Corey Aist, a volunteer member of Alaska Search and Rescue Dogs in Anchorage, Alaska. Corey explains how blizzards keep rescuers and dogs like his golden Labrador, Vanilla Bean, busy finding people buried in snow avalanches—and how he almost became a victim of an avalanche himself!

Whenever I hear there's going to be a blizzard, my first thought is always "Avalanche!"

It happened to me. I was an assistant teacher with a class backcountry in an area near Anchorage. It was still snowing and there had been lots of accumulation from an earlier blizzard, but we'd put ourselves in what we thought was a pretty safe area.

Then all those tons and tons of snow came down right above us. We were hit by what we call a blast (a shock wave of air that gets pushed in front of a rushing avalanche) and I felt the wind coming off it and all the snow kicked up. Afterwards there was snow everywhere—the kitchen was buried. We had to come back with a metal detector to dig out what we could.

Even someone who should know better can get in a situation like that.

Kid Quiz

Q: What's a whiteout?

A: Many people use the word "whiteout" to talk about times when there is so much blowing snow it is almost impossible to see. But that word is also used to describe what can happen when snow on the ground reflects light. You may not realize it, but shadows help your eyes see how far away things are as well as the shape of objects in the snow. In whiteout conditions, the snow reflects light so brightly, few shadows can be seen. Without them, it's easy for people to lose their sense of balance and direction and they can become lost in the snow.

Tell Me More

In 1998, a terrible ice storm affected millions of people across the northeast United States and southeast Canada. When the storm was over, many of them posted notes about their thoughts and feelings online at a Web site set up just for that. Here are a few excerpted from e-mails written by kids living in Maine, one of the U.S. states hardest hit:

I was looking out the window the first day of the ice storm. Huge trees were falling everywhere. On the telephone pole in front of my house, the transformer blew up and a ball of flame burst out of it with a big pop. Instantly the power went out and the ball of flame disappeared on the ground. I will never forget that!

- Ten years old
Woodside Elementary School, Topsham, ME

The hardest part of the storm was missing so much school and having to move from place to place, and not knowing where you were going to sleep that night or if you would have clean clothing the next day or if you would have to wear the same smelly clothes that you had worn the past four days.

- Thirteen years old

Falmouth Middle School, Falmouth, ME

On the first bitter cold, icy morning, I heard we had no school, I thought it was great. The driveway was like a big ice skating rink and my yard was perfect for sledding down. As the ice storm went on my family was beginning to get frustrated; it came to the point were everyone around us had power except us. My dad attached a spotlight from the lighter in our car and brought it in the house. It took us a while to get adjusted to seeing some sort of light again.

- Fourteen years old
Massabesic High School, Limerick, ME

—From "Community of Learners Network" at www.col.k12.me.us/icestorm hosted by Jim Moulton

Taken by Storm

Ice storms, like the one in 1998, can be just as dangerous as blizzards—just ask nine-year-old Natasha Dilkie of Stittsville, Canada:

It sounded like thousands of people blowing on our house and outside everything was totally white. Trees were bending in half because of all the ice, and sharp icicles were hanging down. It was really beautiful outside, but deadly. I wasn't allowed to play under the trees because the ice could fall and kill me.

We didn't have power for five days and it was pretty scary at night. My mom would always put a candle in my room but blow it out when we went to bed. It was very dark and you could hear trees crashing in the forest.

Natasha's dad, Lee, remembers one especially close call:

We'd hear a big crack *every five or ten minutes and then a sound like broken glass, tons of panes of glass, crashing to the ground. And then this big tree fell, with only a power line holding it off our house. The tree was threatening to pull the line right off the pole so I had to knock some ice off. I whacked it with a stick—a hockey stick, I think—and there was all this ice falling on me. It hurt! But it was the prettiest destruction I ever saw. It was like living in a crystal palace, everything sparkling like diamonds . . . like something in a fairy tale.*

6

Winter Storm Survival

The radio crackles with static, then a voice announces: "Blizzard Warning!" In this chapter, you'll learn what to do when watches and warnings are issued.

A Killer Storm

Most injuries and deaths during winter storms result from accidents on ice and snow-slick streets. A lot of injuries also result through exposure to the cold. Such exposure can lead to **hypothermia** and **frostbite**.

Overexertion from shoveling or walking in deep snow is another big reason behind blizzard casualties. That kind of effort can cause a heart attack—or it can simply cause people to sweat, which makes them more susceptible to a bad chill or hypothermia.

Danger! Danger!

Stay tuned to reports from the National Weather Service, local news agencies, and media outlets such as The Weather Channel. Different parts of the country use different types of advisories and warnings. Here is a list of the ones used most commonly today and what they mean. You can find out even more by visiting a site online dedicated to storm safety. "Project Safeside" can be found on the web at www.weather.com/safeside.

Winter Storm Watch

A watch indicates that significant winter weather is possible, including heavy snow, **sleet,** or **freezing rain.** It is usually issued twenty-four to forty-eight hours before the storm is expected to hit. Now is the time to prepare. This means making sure you have all you need for what may be a long, and even cold, stay.

Winter Storm Warning

A warning lets you know that significant

KID QUIZ

Q: How do you get hypothermia?

A: When a person's whole body temperature is lowered by long exposure to the cold. it's called hypothermia. Some symptoms are shivering that just won't stop. and a feeling of sleepiness or dizziness. Frostbite is also a danger with hypothermia. That's what happens when tissues in the skin die off from the cold. People with hypothermia and frostbite shouldn't be rubbed to be kept warm. Instead. call a doctor or hospital for help. They may instruct you to wrap the frost-bitten person in blankets or submerge the freezing areas in warm water.

weather is about to arrive or is happening now. Try to stay indoors. Keep travel to a minimum. Keep up with the latest weather information.

Winter Weather Advisory
This is what you'll hear when winter weather is expected to cause some inconvenience but if caution is used, it should not be life-threatening. An advisory is not as severe as a "watch" or "warning."

Blizzard Warning
When you hear this warning, don't leave home if you don't absolutely have to. If the visibility reduction is not expected to meet the criteria for a blizzard, but a thick covering is predicted, some areas will issue a heavy snow warning or advisory instead.

Freezing Rain/Sleet/Ice Storm
When it looks like you'll see one of these variations of icy precipitation, you should

stay inside, depending on the specific conditions in your area

Wind Chill Warnings and Advisories
These types of alerts are issued when **wind chill factors** are going to plunge to thirty-five degrees below zero or worse. You should try to avoid going out at all when there's this type of warning, but if you must, bundle up every inch of exposed skin or you'll experience frost bite and other cold-related symptoms after just a few minutes.

Building a Disaster Kit

The Red Cross and other organizations suggest that every family collect a kit to carry them through a blizzard or other natural disaster. Doing it before there's any danger is a good idea. Here's what you should have handy:

•A full change of clothes and one blanket

or sleeping bag for each person

•A first-aid kit plus any prescription medications members of your family usually take

•A battery-powered NOAA Weather Radio (a radio specially tuned to carry stations broadcast by the National Oceanographic and Atmospheric Administration, the people who bring you all those weather warnings) and a regular portable radio

•A flashlight

•Lots of extra batteries in sizes that fit all the things in your kit

•An extra set of car keys

•Any special things needed by members of the family—think about the needs of people who are older, disabled, or very young

Car kits should include all of the above, plus: a knife; an empty can with a tight lid and tissues (to use in place of a toilet); a waterproof package of matches to melt snow for water; a sack of sand or kitty litter to put under sliding wheels; a tow rope; a tool kit; booster cables; compass and road maps; windshield scraper and brush; plus a container of water.

Caught in the Crossfire

What happens if you are caught in a winter storm? The first rule is to stay where you are if you're in a house or car. Otherwise, look for some kind of shelter.

WHEN STRANDED IN A CAR OR TRUCK . . .

Stay there! If you leave, you could easily get lost in the snow, even if you think you know the way. It's also easier for rescuers to spot a car than a person, but you can help by tying some bright fabric to the antenna and turning on the inside light at night. Move around as much as you can inside the car to keep the warm blood flowing.

WHEN SNOWBOUND AT HOME OR IN ANOTHER BUILDING . . .

Stay inside! If you lose power, bundle up in layers of clothes, huddle together in just a few rooms, and close all doors. Seal out the cold by stuffing towels or rags under doors and around windows, and by covering windows at night. If you have another source of heat, like a fireplace, or battery-powered space heater, be very careful when using it.

WHEN CAUGHT OUTSIDE . . .

If you can't find a shelter, build one!

KID QUIZ

Q: Why do people put salt on snow?

A: Salt actually lowers the freezing point of water, so it can melt both snow and ice when the temperatures aren't too cold.

Collect fallen branches to create a structure that leans against a boulder, tree or other large object so it can act as a windbreak where you'll be protected from the worst gusts and blowing snow.

Did You Know?

If you're snowbound by a blizzard and get thirsty, it's not a good idea to eat snow. It lowers your body temperature, making it easier for you to get hypothermia and frostbite. If you melt the snow first, you won't have a problem.

GLOSSARY

AIR MASS—A very large body of air, roughly the same temperature and humidity throughout its area; such masses may be cold and dry, warm and moist, or other combinations

AVALANCHE—A dangerous slide of snow or other debris down a slope

BLIZZARD—A winter storm in which sustained wind or frequent gusts of thirty-five miles an hour or more combine with falling and/or blowing snow to reduce visibility to 1/4 mile or less for at least three hours

FREEZING RAIN—A form of precipitation that occurs when snowflakes melt and then refreeze into ice upon reaching the ground

FRONT—The boundary between two different air masses; weather can be very changeable in its vicinity

FROSTBITE—A condition brought on by

exposure to the cold; skin tissues freeze and die

GLAZE—A layer of ice that has very little air trapped in it so it appears clear

HAIL—An ice crystal that forms in a thunderstorm, then becomes a large pellet after being coated with layer after layer of additional ice

HYPOTHERMIA—A condition in which overall body temperature is dangerously lowered through exposure to the cold; unless warmed, a person could die

ICE CRYSTAL—A six-sided form of solid water; the building blocks for snowflakes

ICE STORM (glaze storm)—A weather pattern that produces significant or damaging amounts of freezing rain

JET STREAM—A band of strong wind that circles the Earth around 30,000 feet up in the air; the jet stream helps to steer and energize storms

LOW PRESSURE SYSTEM (depression)—An area of low air pressure in the atmosphere, usually producing winds and precipitation (sunny, quiet weather generally (but not always!) occurs with areas of high pressure)

PHOTOMICROGRAPHS—Photographs of tiny objects taken using special equipment that combines a camera and microscope

PRECIPITATION—Water that falls from the sky and reaches the ground in forms such as rain, snow or ice pellets

SLEET—A form of precipitation that occurs when snowflakes melt and then refreeze into pellets of ice before reaching the ground

WATER VAPOR—Water in the form of an invisible gas

WIND CHILL FACTOR—The combination of cold air and wind makes exposed skin feel colder than if the conditions were calm

INDEX